This book belongs to
....

Copyright © 2024 Kate Pricklewood
All rights reserved.
ISBN: 978-1-0685583-2-0

The Hedgehog Family's Silly Snow Day

Kate Pricklewood

Once upon a time, in their cozy burrow on the edge of the great forest, lived a curious and fun-loving family of hedgehogs. There was Daddy Hedgehog, who was strong, wise, and famous for getting his paws stuck in places they shouldn't be (like the honey jar); Mommy Hedgehog, who was sweet, caring, and could make the best hot chocolate in the world (with extra marshmallows, of course); and their three children — Holly, Henry, and Hazel — who were always ready for an adventure, especially when it involved getting messy!

One chilly winter morning, the hedgehog family woke up to a magical surprise. The forest outside was covered in a thick, sparkling blanket of snow! The trees were dusted white, the air was crisp, and the whole world looked like a giant, fluffy snowball.

"Wow!" squealed Holly, leaning out the window. "Look at all that snow! It's perfect for building snow hedgehogs!"

Henry waddled to the door and tried to open it, but it was stuck. "Uh-oh," he said, "I think we're snowed in!" Daddy Hedgehog chuckled. "Don't worry, I've got this!" He puffed up his chest like he was about to move a mountain, grabbed the handle, and yanked the door with all his strength. Instead of opening... *BOOM!* Daddy Hedgehog's feet slipped, and he went flying backward, landing in a pile of acorns.

"Well, I've found the acorn stash!" he said, grinning as acorns rolled everywhere, one even stuck on his nose.

Mommy Hedgehog giggled and handed him a broom. "Good find, dear. But next time, let's try pulling like we're opening a door, not yanking a tree out of the ground... Now, let's get bundled up and head outside!"

Soon, the whole family was wrapped up in warm clothes. They waddled out into the snow, leaving little hedgehog prints behind them. Hazel immediately flopped onto her back, waving her paws and feet to make a snow angel. "Look!" Hazel said proudly. "It's a snow-hedgehog angel!"

Holly and Henry giggled as they started to roll snowballs, which grew bigger and bigger. "Let's make a snow hedgehog!" Henry said.
They worked together, stacking one big snowball on top of another, then added twigs for arms, a carrot for the nose and pine needles for the prickles.

"Hey, it looks just like me!" Daddy said, puffing out his chest. Mommy Hedgehog giggled. "It does, except this one won't eat all the nut bread!"

After building their snow hedgehog, the children decided it was time for a snowball fight. Holly, Henry, and Hazel scooped up pawfuls of snow and started tossing snowballs at each other. Daddy Hedgehog tried to hide behind a tree, but *splat!* — a snowball hit him right on the nose.

"Hey!" Daddy Hedgehog said, laughing. "You little snow rascals!"

Mommy Hedgehog, who had been watching with a smile, suddenly scooped up her own snowball and tossed it at Daddy. *Splat!* It hit him right on the back.

"Now you're in trouble!" Daddy Hedgehog declared playfully. He grabbed a pile of snow and made the biggest snowball ever. "Incoming!"

Daddy Hedgehog's huge snowball sailed through the air, aiming straight for Mommy Hedgehog. She gasped and quickly ducked behind the snow hedgehog the children had built. *Splat!* The giant snowball missed her by an inch and exploded into a fluffy shower of snowflakes.

"Nice try!" Mommy Hedgehog called, peeking out from her snowy shield. She scooped up more snow and quickly fired back, sending snowballs whizzing toward Daddy Hedgehog, who dodged and laughed.

The children squealed with delight. "Team up on Daddy!" Holly shouted, and all three kids began launching snowballs at him from every direction.
"Oh no, I'm outnumbered!" Daddy Hedgehog exclaimed dramatically, pretending to stumble as snowballs landed on his back, belly, and paws. "You've got me!"

Just then, Henry had an idea. "Let's build a snow fort!" he cried, gathering snow into little walls.
Holly and Hazel quickly joined in, and soon they had created a small fort to defend against Daddy's snowball barrage. The kids ducked behind the walls, popping up occasionally to throw more snowballs while giggling uncontrollably.
Daddy Hedgehog pretended to plan his next move, pacing around like a general. "I'll break through your defenses! No snow fort is safe from me!"

But before he could launch his next attack, Mommy Hedgehog sneaked up behind him with a snowball in each paw. "Oh no you don't!" she teased, gently tossing both snowballs at his back.
Splat, splat!
Daddy Hedgehog laughed, surrendering to the playful ambush. "Okay, okay, you win!"

Daddy collapsed into the snow, breathless from laughter, snowflakes clinging to his prickles. Holly, Henry, and Hazel dancing around him, cheering, "We did it! We beat Daddy!" Mommy Hedgehog smiled down at them. "Looks like we have some snowball champions!"

Daddy Hedgehog smiled, wrapping his arms around the little hedgehogs. "Next time, I'll wear a snowball-proof suit! But for now... who wants hot chocolate?"
The children's eyes lit up. "Me! Me!" they shouted, jumping to their feet and shaking off the snow.

"Best. Snowball. Fight. Ever!" cried Henry.
With smiles on their faces, the Hedgehog family headed back to their cozy burrow.

Back inside the cozy burrow, Mommy Hedgehog made the biggest mugs of hot chocolate ever seen, each one topped with a mountain of marshmallows.
Daddy Hedgehog even managed to dunk a cookie into his hot chocolate without getting crumbs stuck in his prickles — a real victory!

As they gathered around, sipping their hot chocolate, Henry suddenly asked, "Do you think snow hedgehogs come to life at night?"

Daddy Hedgehog grinned. "Well, I've never seen one move, but who knows? Maybe tonight, they'll sneak around and have their own snowball fight!"

The children's eyes widened with excitement. "Maybe we'll catch them in action!" Holly said. "We just have to stay up all night and watch!"

Mommy Hedgehog chuckled. "Good luck with that, my little adventurers, but something tells me you'll be fast asleep before that happens."

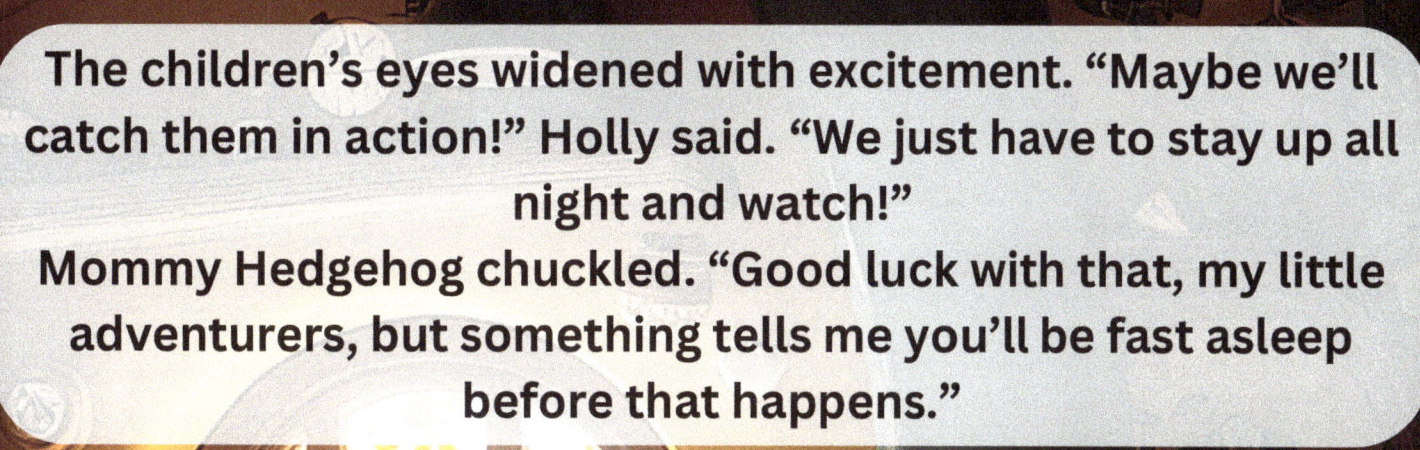

And of course, she was right. After all the snowy fun, the hedgehog children soon snuggled into bed, yawning and dreaming of snowball fights and snow hedgehogs that came to life.

And with that, the cozy little burrow was filled with dreams of snowflakes, snowballs, and sweet hot chocolate until the next grand adventure.

Daddy Hedgehog

Strong and playful, Daddy Hedgehog is always ready for a challenge — though he tends to get himself into funny situations, like flying backward while trying to open a door or getting snowballs stuck to his prickles. He loves to make his children laugh and isn't afraid of a little mischief. Though he pretends to be tough, he's a softie at heart, wrapping his arms around his little ones after every playful snowball fight.

Mommy Hedgehog

Sweet and nurturing, Mommy Hedgehog is the glue that keeps the family together. She has a gentle sense of humor, always ready with a playful quip, whether handing Daddy a broom after his tumble or tossing a snowball at him during the family's snowball fight. Her hot chocolate, topped with extra marshmallows, is legendary, and she brings warmth and love into every activity the family shares.

Holly

Holly is the creative and adventurous eldest child. She's always the first to dive into new adventures, like flopping down in the snow to make a perfect snow-hedgehog angel. Her imagination is boundless, and she often leads her siblings in new games. She's thoughtful, too, wondering about snow hedgehogs coming to life at night.

Henry

Henry is the energetic and inventive middle child, always ready to lead the charge into a snowball fight or come up with a clever idea like building a snow fort to outwit Daddy in their playful battles. He's a bit of a dreamer, fascinated by the idea that snow hedgehogs might come to life when no one's watching. With his boundless curiosity, Henry is always imagining new ways to turn everyday moments into magical adventures.

Hazel

The youngest of the three, Hazel is a bundle of joy who loves to join in on the fun. She's quick to giggle and even quicker to help her siblings with whatever adventure they've cooked up — whether it's rolling snowballs or joining forces to pelt Daddy with snow. Though small, she's full of energy and always has a twinkle in her eye, eager to be part of every family moment.

www.ingramcontent.com/pod-product-compliance
Lightning Source LLC
LaVergne TN
LVHW072114060526
838200LV00061B/4888